The
World's Biggest
Banana

by Sean Julian and Ian Smith

W
FRANKLIN WATTS
LONDON•SYDNEY

First published in 2009 by
Franklin Watts
338 Euston Road
London
NW1 3BH

Franklin Watts Australia
Level 17/207 Kent Street
Sydney
NSW 2000

A CIP catalogue record for this book is available
from the British Library.

ISBN 978 0 7496 9188 2 (hbk)
ISBN 978 0 7496 9194 3 (pbk)

Series Editor: Jackie Hamley
Editor: Melanie Palmer
Series Advisor: Dr Barrie Wade
Series Designer: Peter Scoulding

Printed in China

Franklin Watts is a division of
Hachette Children's Books,
an Hachette UK company.
www.hachette.co.uk

A group of friends,
a hungry bunch,

were searching the
jungle for their lunch.

3

They stopped beneath
a banana tree

4

and were amazed by
what they could see:

a banana of such

enormous size

the friends could hardly
believe their eyes!

Greedily, they

began to say

how they'd eat the fruit

their favourite way.

Monkey's eyes were
brightly lit,

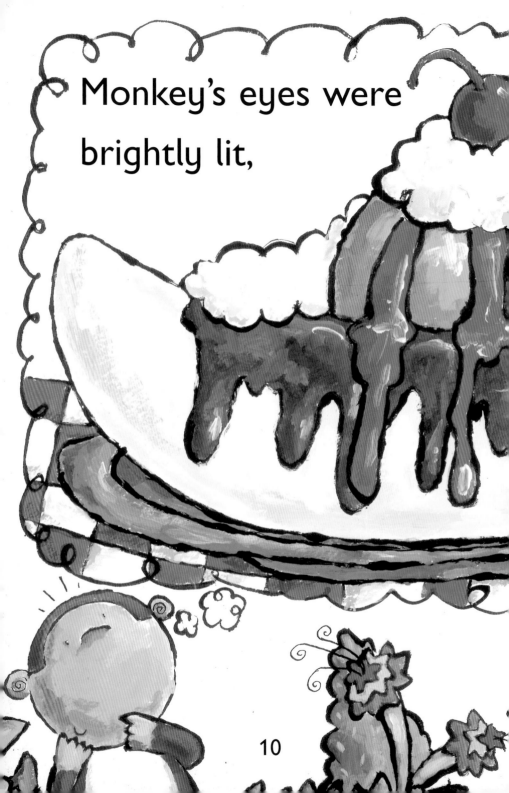

10

"I'll make a huge
banana split!"

Zebra gave his head
a shake,

12

"I'll make a giant banana cake."

Hippo thought that
wouldn't do,

"I'll chop it up and make a stew."

15

Giraffe cried,

"Don't be so hasty!

Banana bread – that's
much more tasty."

17

As the jungle friends
began to squabble,

the ground and trees
began to wobble.

Then they saw
a hairy shape ...

that belonged to the

world's biggest ape!

"This banana,"
said the giant beast,

"is perfect for my
lunchtime feast."

All he left was the

banana skin,

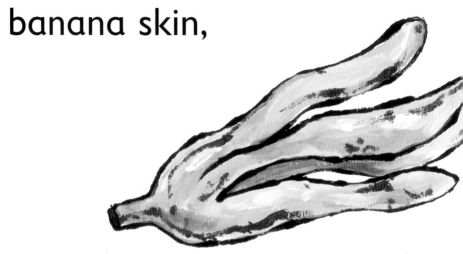

and he walked away
with a happy grin.

The friends were all
left feeling sad,

when they thought of
what they could have had.

A giant banana
is very rare.

They should
have all agreed
to share.

28

Puzzle 1

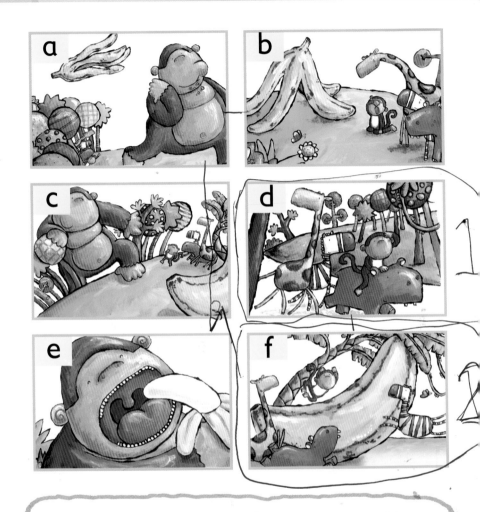

Put these pictures in the correct order.
Now retell the story in your own words.
Is there a lesson in the story?

Puzzle 2

treat	taste
sweet	eat

bath	stew
menu	zoo

bake	ache
bite	cake

Find the non-rhyming word in each word box. Can you think of some words to rhyme with the odd one out?

Answers

Puzzle 1

The correct order is: 1d, 2f, 3c, 4e, 5a, 6b.

Puzzle 2

The odd words out are:

taste, bath, bite

Look out for more Leapfrog Rhyme Time:

Mr Spotty's Potty
ISBN 978 0 7496 3813 3

Freddie's Fears
ISBN 978 0 7496 4382 9

Eight Enormous Elephants
ISBN 978 0 7496 4634 9

Squeaky Clean
ISBN 978 0 7496 6805 1

Felicity Floss: Tooth Fairy
ISBN 978 0 7496 6807 5

Captain Cool
ISBN 978 0 7496 6808 2

Monster Cake
ISBN 978 0 7496 6809 9

The Super Trolley Ride
ISBN 978 0 7496 6810 5

The Royal Jumble Sale
ISBN 978 0 7496 6811 2

But, Mum!
ISBN 978 0 7496 6812 9

Dan's Gran's Goat
ISBN 978 0 7496 6814 3

Lighthouse Mouse
ISBN 978 0 7496 6815 0

Big Bad Bart
ISBN 978 0 7496 6816 7

Ron's Race
ISBN 978 0 7496 6817 4

Boris the Spider
ISBN 978 0 7496 7791 6

Miss Polly's Seaside Brolly
ISBN 978 0 7496 7792 3

The Lonely Pirate
ISBN 978 0 7496 7793 0

Alfie the Sea Dog
ISBN 978 0 7496 7958 3

Red Riding Hood Rap
ISBN 978 0 7496 7959 0

Pets on Parade
ISBN 978 0 7496 7960 6

Let's Dance
ISBN 978 0 7496 7961 3

Benny and the Monster
ISBN 978 0 7496 7962 0

Bathtime Rap
ISBN 978 0 7496 7963 7

Woolly the Bully
ISBN 978 0 7496 7098 6*
ISBN 978 0 7496 7790 9

What a Frog!
ISBN 978 0 7496 7102 0*
ISBN 978 0 7496 7794

Juggling Joe
ISBN 978 0 7496 7103 7*
ISBN 978 0 7496 7795 4

I Wish!
ISBN 978 0 7496 7940 8*
ISBN 978 0 7496 7952 1

Raindrop Bill
ISBN 978 0 7496 7941 5*
ISBN 978 0 7496 7953 8

Sir Otto
ISBN 978 0 7496 7942 2*
ISBN 978 0 7496 7954 5

Queen Rosie
ISBN 978 0 7496 7943 9*
ISBN 978 0 7496 7955 2

Giraffe's Good Game
ISBN 978 0 7496 7944 6*
ISBN 978 0 7496 7956 9

Miss Lupin's Motorbike
ISBN 978 0 7496 7945 3*
ISBN 978 0 7496 7957 6

*hardback

For more Leapfrog books go to: www.franklinwatts.co.uk